Cleaning Out the Closet

Also by Mary Pomfret and published by Ginninderra Press
Writing in Virginia's Shadow

Mary Pomfret

Cleaning Out the Closet

Acknowledgements

Australian Journal of Adoption Vol. 3, No. 2 (2011): 'Cleaning
Out the Closet' (under pen name Mia Francis)

Idiom 23 Vol. 17 (2005): 'Mother Superior's Garden Party'
(Highly Commended, Bauhinia Literary Awards 2004)

The Irish Heritage Journal of Australia (2005):
'Mother Superior's Garden Party'

Idiom 23 Vol. 18 (2006): 'Peripheral Vision'

Scintillae (2012): 'Peripheral Vision'

Thirst (2007): 'Our Darker Purpose'

Radio NAG *Words and Music* (2006): 'Gravy and Tragedy'

Radio Adelaide *Writers and Writing* (2006): 'Gravy and Tragedy'

Tamba (2006): 'Gravy and Tragedy' (Highly Commended,
C.J. Dennis Literary Awards 2004)

Wakefield Press, *Culture is…* (2008): a version of 'Gravy
and Tragedy' appears as 'Walking Shoes'

Arabesques Review (2007): 'Eulogy for a Myth'

Hecate (2009): 'Verification' (under pen name Mia Francis)

Idiom 23 Vol. 20 (2008) 'Venus'

Hecate (2006): 'La Tristesse'

Pendulum Issue 8 (2004): 'Brother' (First Prize, Port Phillip
Citizens for Reconciliation Literary Award 2003)

For John and Eric

Cleaning Out the Closet
ISBN 978 1 74027 856 0

Cover image: Kathryn Harrison, *Pumpkin*, 2013

First published 2014
Reprinted 2015

GINNINDERRA PRESS
PO Box 3461 Port Adelaide 5015
www.ginninderrapress.com.au

Contents

… I thought how unpleasant it is to be locked out;
and I thought how it is worse perhaps to be locked in…
– Virginia Woolf, 1928

Cleaning Out the Closet

She gazed at the peeling wallpaper – teddy bears playing drums and trumpets, arms and legs frozen in the motion of marching to the silent beat of a childhood tune. More of it just seemed to peel away each year. Ricky had never asked for it to be taken down. His girlfriends all seemed to like it, but now the teddies were marching their final march. Tomorrow she would paint his room.

She blew the dust off the box of Lego blocks as she lifted it from the bottom of the closet. Rose paused for a moment from her task, her back stiff from bending for so long. 'Do you want this old Lego?' she called to him down the hallway.

'And what would I do with old Lego, Mum?' he called back.

At breakfast earlier, she'd said to him, 'Ricky, just an observation, not a criticism, but I have noticed that you seem a lot more relaxed now that you've finished your degree and you have a job to go to… now that everything's finalised.' As soon as she uttered the words she wished she hadn't. She knew instantly by the furrowing of his brow that she had annoyed him.

'Oh have you, Mum? And who are you? The narrator?' he'd said with a mouthful of toast. 'You know, Mum, you have narrated my life for me since I was three. Every time I do anything, you have to tell me about it. I really don't want to hear your version of my life any more, especially in those plays you write.'

She laughed. 'Can I have that last line?'

'No…not unless you pay me for it,' he said. His frown had disappeared.

He was leaving. He was going to Canberra. He would be back from time to time, but he was leaving. Like the fool in the Tarot card deck, he was on his way. If she faced it, he was gone already.

When she scraped off the wallpaper tomorrow, she would keep one small square and put it in a frame. How Ricky would laugh at her when he saw it. Mum, you and your sacred relics, he would say. She thought about the faded little drawing that hung on her bedroom wall. How she treasured that little artwork. Although she had framed it, the glass pane had not stopped the fading and each year it got a little lighter. Bits of it had faded more than others. It was a simple one-dimensional drawing of a house with one door, two windows and chimney with smoke blowing out – you know the type that five-year-olds do. Across the top of his drawing Ricky had written in his very best printing, 'Mum Your Home'. A few months ago, she had decided to take it down to photocopy it before it became too faded. When she'd hung it back on the bedroom wall, she'd noticed that part of it had faded entirely. The stick figure, her son in self-portrait, five-year-old style, who had stood along the side of the house, had disappeared entirely. Is that how children fade from our lives? Is it when we least expect it? Then she wondered if she had deceived herself, imagined it. Perhaps he had never been in the picture at all.

She glanced again at the peeling teddies and the growing pile of discards in the corner of his room: broken toys, old textbooks, tatty folders of notes, odd socks, old soccer boots, a broken bike pump, a once-treasured Pokémon collection and now a shoebox full of old Lego. Rose had been cleaning for most of the morning and her legs were beginning to feel stiff from all the bending and reaching into far corners. She sat down on the edge of Ricky's bed to rest for a moment or two. She arched her back, stretched and looked up at the ceiling at the cobwebs in the corners.

Thinking back to a scene from her own disappearance, her own leaving home, she could see her father standing with his back to the open fire in the kitchen as was always his habit in the cold winter. He was standing there like this the night she told him that she was leaving. Did he feel then as she did now?

'I'm going to Western Australia tomorrow, Dad.'

She remembered he looked down at his feet and he didn't say anything for a long while.

'Well, do you want me come as far as Melbourne with you?'

'No, Dad. I'll be okay.'

Did she say goodbye to him before she left? Perhaps that had been their goodbye, those few words in front of the fire. He'd said to her years later nothing can really prepare for that unexpected moment when your child tells you that they are leaving. She recalled the final scene of her departure. The tyres of the taxi had crunched the stones in the driveway as it pulled out. She hadn't looked back.

None of us want our childhoods when we are eighteen. It is something we have to leave behind, move on from as quickly as possible, an embarrassment almost; a skin to be shed, to be cast off. How fragile it all is. How fragile, how fleeting and how careless we all are when we are acting our part, taking our turn. How quickly life becomes memory, like scenes in a play with an ephemeral script that can be replayed at will.

'Mum, what have you done with all my socks?' Ricky called from the laundry.

Rose laughed to herself. Some things never changed. He had never been able to find his socks.

'Well, maybe you wore them for days on end and then they self-destructed,' she called back.

By now he would have tipped the laundry basket upside down on the floor and he would be swearing quietly, hunting through the pile of clean washing.

'Very funny, Mum. You must have put them somewhere. You're always messing around with my stuff. Where the fuck…'

It seemed like just a blink of an eye since she and Tom had pulled up outside the grey stone-walled orphanage to collect their son. She remembered how the adoption worker had mentioned to them that they might offend the locals with their smell. Apparently, Europeans who eat dairy food have a particularly acrid scent to the noses of Asians who don't drink milk or eat cheese. Ricky smelled like lollies to Rose in those first tentative days. In fact, the whole crowded city had a heavy cloying sweetness which seemed particularly oppressive in the humidity of the late afternoons. Even the nuns smelled sweet.

But Rose remembered that at first it was the smallness of him which struck her most. For his three and a half years he was a tiny, elegant little person but so small. He was wearing white shorts with a picture of Homer Simpson on the back, a red and white striped T-shirt and an American baseball cap. The nuns said that this was 'his trousseau'. Had they powdered his face? Perhaps they had, because his face looked so white compared to the rest of him – a pale moon face which seemed too big and round for the rest of his little body. And she picked him up, picked him up for the first time. For Rose, that moment was as if her newborn had been placed on her chest– a mise en scène, a still shot, emblazoned in her memory. Rose was amazed how light he had felt. He clung to her without knowing who she was, where she was from or just what role she was going to play in his life. It was as though there was some innate optimism or hope within him that she would meet his needs; that she would care for him; that she would be his mother.

Rose returned to the editing of childhood accumulations and pulled out a couple of old soccer boots. Ricky had always loved playing with balls. She recalled that she took balloons with her in her luggage because the agency worker had told her that Ricky's case notes reported that he loved playing with anything that moved. The lightness of the balloons seemed to be so in keeping with the elegance of those delicate little hands. She, Tom and Ricky spent those first early days in a luxurious hotel in Manila and their new son seemed to suffer from disorientation of a kind. When Rose took him to the shopping centre and held his hand, he would tug at her pulling her in the opposite direction crying 'Dun tay uu. (Let's go this way.)' Rose realised later that he didn't have the words for 'Let's go home,' and she was sure that this was what he would have been trying to say. The home he would have meant would have been the grey stone building: the orphanage.

Memories seemed to be tumbling over one another while she was down on her knees retrieving the last of the Lego pieces. She thought now of the first time that she heard Ricky cry. He banged his head on the poolside table, not hard, but hard enough to make him cry. Rose remembered the sound he had made. The word 'cry' was inadequate; it was more like an animal sound, a tearless, low rasping bark. Is that what happens when a child's cry goes unheard, ignored, unnoticed for hours days, months, even years? Does it become a mutated form of itself – a sound of hopeless misery rather than a shrill expectant call for attention? It only came the once, that sound. She had never heard him cry that way since.

And then there was that Friday morning not long after they arrived back in Australia. Funny how she remembered that it was Friday. But that morning was different – there seemed something more intense about his need to be picked up. She didn't put him down to make breakfast. Instead she carried him to the lounge room and turned on the CD player. Pavarotti sang. Ricky tightened his grip around her neck and wrapped his legs around her waist, locking his ankles together. She was very slim in those days and he had long legs. They walked together like that for nearly three hours, up and down the lounge room floor, backwards and forwards, up and down, with Pavarotti stuck on repeat. It was only after the phone rang out three times that she decided to answer it. That time Ricky didn't cry when she put him down. This all seemed like light years ago to Rose now in one way, yet in another it seemed like yesterday.

Another call from the laundry interrupted her thoughts. 'Mum, there are no undies either.'

She looked at a pile of socks and underpants in the corner behind the chair. Rose had been successful in teaching Ricky many things, but doing his washing wasn't one of them. She had taught him to drive, though. Hours of practice, hours of being together in the car, talking, arguing about something or other, and Ricky learning to drive.

She recalled the day they had driven to the Murray River for a long driving lesson. They bought fish and chips and sat on the riverbank watching the river flow and the steamboats paddle by. He sat on one rock and she'd sat on another. Somewhere she had read that the ancients had recognised that certain places are 'thin places'; places where you can feel the past, present and the future; places where the veil between this world and the other is like fine lace.

Ricky turned his back to her, messaging his girlfriend on his mobile phone, eating hot chips, unaware of his beauty, unaware of his own fragility, unaware of her overwhelming love for him at that moment. 'Mum, they didn't give us any tomato sauce for the chips,' he said.

They played Paul Kelly's 'To her Door' all the way home.

'That song makes me homesick,' he said.

Was his script the same as hers after all?

'I know what you mean,' she replied.

It was a song that she played over and over when he was little. She would sit on the back porch with a glass of wine on summer evenings, playing music on an old portable tape deck and watch him riding his scooter, amazed at his simple happiness and joy in just being alive.

Tom said once, before he left her for the last time, 'Boys love their mums and they hang around for a while, but once they're gone they're gone. You've got to accept that, Rose. Just let go. Boys just go.'

Rose tried not to think of Tom often; but as she caught sight of the last little red Lego block wedged in a crack on the floor of the closet, she missed Tom. She missed him, and the part he had played in the story that they had shared.

Loud music jolted Rose back to the cleaning of the Ricky's dusty closet. What was this blasting again? 'When I'm Gone'? Tomorrow even the teddies on the wall would be gone. Loud footsteps echoed down the hall. His tall athletic form filled the doorway.

'Mum, I've got to go in a minute and there's no….' He stopped and looked at her. 'Mum…are you…?'

'It's okay. The narrator's just stuck in a tragic scene.' She wiped her face with the back of her hand.

'You're weird, Mum.'

In just a few hours, after he was gone, she would probably stand for a while in the garden under a tree. Anything to avoid that moment, that moment when she would walk back into the house, bracing herself for the finality of seeing the familiar become unfamiliar, that moment when her home would dissolve into a dwelling, become merely a timber construction with a tin roof, empty of all but furniture and fittings. A strange landscape in which she knew she would no longer fit, no longer have a place. Ricky was still there, he hadn't left yet, but already she could hear the crunch of the tyres on the stones in the driveway. And she knew he wouldn't look back.

Tomorrow she would paint his room.

Mother Superior's Garden Party

'Mother Superior' has her undertaker's voice on her when she leaves the message on my answering machine.

That name for my sister Bridget came to me after an argument we had over a pair of old rosary beads from a market stall. Beautiful old ivory beads they were, the little carved roses worn satin smooth by some poor soul's praying. Now the precious beads hang over Bridget's dressing table mirror alongside her French perfumes and the family pictures.

The message? It is a rare thing that she has called at all. Would I call her back? 'Nothing urgent,' she says in that tone of hers, but if I could call back as soon as possible she would greatly appreciate it.

So what has happened? Is our father finally dead? Or does someone in the family need money and she isn't going to be one to give it?

'Bridget, it's me. Roisin. Is everything okay?'

'Of course. Just letting you know that we'll be giving Mum a garden party for her seventieth birthday this Saturday. Mary and I are arranging it all and the whole family will be there. Pat's coming and we've even asked Dad.'

'So you've got it all organised by the sound of things. Where is it by the way?' I ask.

'It's at James's place – you know James – he has a fabulous old place at Castlemaine – he's always liked Mum. So it's going to be wonderful – an afternoon garden party with champagne and cucumber sandwiches, 1930s style.'

'Sure – see you Saturday, sis,' I say as I hang up the phone.

Short notice serves its own purpose. It is Thursday – two days to make arrangements – just little enough time to make it difficult to get to get there, but long enough to make it not impossible.

On the train, I am conspicuous in my garden party attire. Floral dress, red and yellow roses on black, a hand-me-down from an old hippie friend, hangs loosely around my ankles; resurrected straw hat with a big black velvet bow at the back sits tightly on my head. I feel the hat to check that there are no cobwebs hanging from it. Clutching my little beaded bag with black lace-gloved hands, I hope look the part if nothing else.

'Nice day for it, dear,' says the old lady sitting opposite me in a mauve knitted suit.

Train journey over, I walk down the tree-lined street, shiny black high heels clicking against the cracked concrete pavement, towards James's magnificent but decaying old mansion. Trees coming out from winter's sleep are fresh and beautiful for their spring debut. James has tied a huge yellow ribbon around the massive Indian bean tree at the front of his palace. Standing under the green canopy of heart-shaped leaves and vast tortured branches, I read the little worn metal plaque.

Planted by Edward O'Reilly, in loving memory of his wife
Charity (1865–1881) died in childbirth, aged 16 years.

For a few sweet moments, I breathe in the love.

The street is lined with cars – the red Jaguar will be brother Pat's, I'm sure, and the old Mercedes is sister Mary's, no doubt. Bridget will have come with Mary – my two sisters always arrive and leave together.

I go over on the side of my ankle and just manage to steady myself as Mother Superior herself comes striding down the red brick rose-lined driveway. So lean and leggy she is in her white leather jeans and top, her jet-black hair tied in a sleek Spanish bun and her gold bracelets jangling. White-capped teeth flashing and her violet eyes shining, she says, 'Roisin – you managed to get here. Mum will be pleased.'

'Is Dad here, Bridget?'

'Yes. Isn't it fantastic?'

James comes forward to greet me, gallant as ever. He could be the Great Gatsby himself in his dinner suit, black tie and dazzling white shirt with his blond hair parted in the middle. I think I smell Californian Poppy as he kisses me on the cheek.

'Roisin, darling. Come, let me get you some champagne.' James pours a glass of the best. 'Your brother Pat and your father have supplied twenty bottles,' he says as he hands me the glass.

'Did you know, Roisin, that Napoleon had the traditional champagne glass fashioned after Josephine's breast?' he says in that languid way that he has about him.

'Well no, I didn't know that now, James. You look so handsome today in your dinner suit.'

He smiles back at me – a professional smile maybe, a newsreader's smile possibly, but a smile nonetheless and how I need a smile just now.

My mother, in wheelchair that someone has parked under the magnolia tree, is alone staring into an untouched glass of champagne, a pink crocheted rug on her knees.

'Happy birthday, Mum.'

'Hello, love. It's a nice party, isn't i? Someone's birthday, I think. Did you come far today?'

'It's me – Roisin, Mum. I came on the train for your birthday. 'I hand her a small pink tissue parcel.

'Is it my birthday, dear? I get so mixed up these days. How sweet of you to give me a present. What was your name, dear?'

'It's me – Roisin, Mum. Don't you remember?'

'Thank you, dear,' she says quietly.

'I see Dad's here, Mum – over there by the wisteria.'

'You mean the old man with those lovely young women around him – is that your father, love?'

My father has scrubbed up well for the occasion – always handsome, and in spite of his years his hair is still deep auburn. Sitting with my sisters Bridget and Mary either side of him, he is holding a gypsy court. My brother Pat, standing alongside our father, is like a sentinel. Hero worship is easier than facing the truth, it seems – much easier.

I watch my mother's soft white hands twist around the champagne glass and remember another time, a time when they weren't white, but rough and work worn – cracked and stained brown from toil, drudgery and the potatoes.

Potatoes – endless potatoes she would peel night after night, our staple in those lean years. Most often we had them mashed with a kind of gravy and sometimes there were a few carrots and maybe even turnips; sometimes, if my father had had a good week, there might be a few lamb chops for an Irish stew.

Looking across at my father engrossed now in his own hero recounts, I remember the night he came home and flung a huge pot of Irish stew across the kitchen into the fireplace. All afternoon my mother had worked to make that pot of stew that was to last us for the rest of the week, and he, the hero, had flung it into the fireplace. I see it now, the few precious chops clinging to the bricks and the carrots and potatoes all over the hearth; the hearth that my mother had scrubbed clean that day.

'You,' he had screamed at me, 'you, ya fecking nitwit – clean up this fecking mess before I kick you to kingdom come.'

Something deep within me burns with that memory.

Bridget, Mary and little Pat, asleep and tucked up in bed by my mother long before my father's return, knew none of this. It was me, the chosen one, chosen to wait with her, to defend her, to bear witness to these secret tragedies and to never tell; to never breathe a word.

A soft breeze blows and I bend and kiss my mother. I walk across to greet my father. 'Hello, Dad.'

'Oh, so it's you again. How are you, my love – any complaints?'

'Do you think that I should have a complaint, Dad?'

'You always have a complaint, Roisin – so what is it this time? By the way, have you thanked your sisters for arranging this lovely do for your mother?'

'No, Dad, but I guess I'll get around to it.'

My sisters stare at me, smiling with their perfectly capped teeth.

Mary jumps up, wafting expensive perfume and kisses our father's head. 'Dad, let me get you some sandwiches and champagne,' she says and Mother Superior pats his hand.

Pat, my brother, standing nearby, soldier-like, speaks softly, 'How are you doing there, Da'? You feeling okay?'

I look up and see a stranger, a stranger who had been my little brother once.

'Ah Pat, I'm fine, son, just fine. Now do you remember that old codger who lived on the corner – what was his name now – yes, that's it – the Shadow they used to call him, wasn't it – he used to go berserk every Friday night …' My father drones on, his hypnotic voice demanding attention.

He loves to tell a story, does my father and today will be no different.

'It's a self-educated man I am, you know. But if there is one thing I can't stand it's a braggart. Nothing worse than a braggart,' he says. 'I brought your mother to this country when she was sixteen, and it was penniless I was then – penniless but not useless. Isn't that true, Kathleen? Wheel your mother over here, Roisin.'

My mother, still holding her champagne glass, is on a cloud somewhere in that blue sky as her soft eyes stare smilingly through my father.

'Oh no, it was far from useless I was. The fecking hard way it was that I made my money. Kathleen, you would remember that now. None of your airs and graces about it – just bloody hard work and sweat.'

He stops and looks at my mother. 'Are you keeping well these days, Kathleen, my love.'

My mother, still floating on a cloud, closes her eyes.

'I hope you've been looking after your mother, Roisin. Not spending all your time mooning over your romance books and such, I hope. You and your fanciful ways – it's loving care and attention that your mother needs now that she's ailing. Do they teach you that at your precious university, Roisin?'

'No, Dad, I don't believe they do teach us loving care and attention as you put it. And where was it that you learnt all your loving ways, Dad?'

'Oh, so it's turning nasty you are now, is it? It doesn't take you long, does it?'

'Roisin, why is that you have to cause trouble at every family occasion that you come to? If you don't like us, then don't come. That old chip just gets wider, doesn't it?' Sister Mary says.

'Yes. Just don't come, Roisin, if that's the way you feel. Just don't come. Da', let me take your plate. Now, what was that story you started about the man and the whiskey bottle?' Mother Superior says.

'Oh yes, darlin', that was it,' and he smiles broadly. 'It was the time…' and his harsh Irish brogue drifts high into the trees as I walk away.

As I look back over my shoulder, Mother Superior is taking my mother, Kathleen, back over to the magnolia tree.

'My mother's tired, James. Be a love and call her a cab,' I hear Mother Superior say.

Oh yes, tired she might well be by now, my mother. Tired of listening to the my father's valiant reminiscences, heroic tales of how he made his millions in a strange and harsh country with no one to back him save his own faith and courage. Yes, tales of how he started with but a single market stall and now directs his own company – such was his tenacity and strength. Oh yes, and tired of watching the hapless, unquestioning adoration of his children. Tired she might well be feeling now, my mother.

The memory of her hands comes back to me again. The deep red cracks that she used to cover with lanolin and the brown stains she tried to bleach with lemon juice. How many potatoes had they peeled, those hands?

But there are no hero's tales to be found in peeling potatoes – none at all, it seems. Mascara tears bleed down my cheeks. I run down the red-brick, rose-lined path towards the gate. My stiletto catches in the bricks on the path. I bend to retrieve it and James touches my hand.

Smiling, he gives me back my shoe. 'Let me walk you to the Indian bean tree, Roisin.'

Peripheral Vision

The old fly-wire door springs open and bangs back against the wall.

Alice rushes in and flings her schoolbag down with a thud on the wooden floorboards. 'Mum, guess what? You'll never guess,' she gushes. 'I was a bullseye today, Mum. A bull's-eye!'

'And what may I ask is a bullseye? And shut the door – you're letting all the flies in,' I say.

'A bullseye, Mum,' says Alice, pulling herself up to her full height, 'is someone who is always at the centre of things, a person who everyone likes. We had to do this chart and say where we belonged in the group at school. I put myself right in the middle. That's me there, see,' she says, holding her chart and pointing. 'All the nerds and dorky kids put themselves on the very outside ring. I reckon they did that just to make everyone feel sorry for them.'

I open the fridge and see the can of beer sitting there, beckoning me like a friend. I take it out and pull back the ring top. Three thirty-five – a bit early maybe. Lois, my neighbour, had offered me one for morning tea last Saturday. Nothing too unusual in Darwin.

'Some kids can't help being dorks – I think I was one,' I say.

She hasn't heard me, and I'm glad.

She skips down the passage, blonde curls bobbing. 'Just ringing Susie, Mum,' she calls.

Me at her age – long, dark lanky locks, skinny legs, hand-me-down school uniform, too short. Nothing like my little princess with her shining curls and heart-shaped dimpled face.

I pour the beer into a frosty glass and wipe the sweat from my oily face with the wet flannel I keep in the fridge. No chance of wearing make-up at this time of year. Clouds are building outside and the smell of the fickle rain is in the air. I take a gulp of beer, lick the frothy moustache from my upper lip and begin flouring the barramundi for tea.

Later, when Alice is softly sleeping, I sit on the creaky old cane chair on the front veranda. Now onto my second glass of red for the evening, I take a long sip. The cicadas are louder than usual tonight. The fetid humid air that has settled on me, weighs down on me, takes hold. The booze helps.

As always, I start thinking of Jim. It was okay at first, I guess, but it got so that he was drunk most of the time. I don't think he even knew who I was in the end, or even cared, for that matter. It was when he started peeing in the corner in the middle of the night that I couldn't stand it any more. He must have known, because one morning he just got up, packed his bag, got in his ute and never came back. Didn't even take his dog. Two years it's been now. Sometimes it's hard to know if I've been any happier since we've been apart. Lonely with him, lonely without him.

When was the last time anyone invited me out? There was the Tupperware party last month, the wine and cheese night at the school at the end of last year and, oh yes, the book club, of course. But never any personal invitations. If the phone rings at all these days, it's for Alice, or the library to let me know my books are over-due.

But life won't be like that for Alice. She won't live on the periphery, always skirting around the edges, making the best of things, waiting for things to get better. No. Not Alice.

Will anyone ever ask me out anywhere again? I look down at my cracked heels and my unpainted toenails. I used to despise feet like these – old duck's feet, I would have called them once. Old duck's feet – don't-care-any-more-feet. I slide my worn thongs off and fan my dress between my legs. The cicadas are getting louder. Must be their mating cry – their love song.

My friend Maggie says, 'You can always tell if a woman is sexually active by her feet. No woman in her right mind would go to bed with a man without her toenails painted.' Maggie's toenails are always painted a glossy red to match her perfectly manicured hands.

The cicadas are deafening now and I swat a mosquito on my arm. It's drawn blood. I wipe my forehead with the back of my hand and pick up a book from the table, the latest highbrow offering from the book club. A new, up-and-coming author, apparently. Maggie said it's rich in symbolism and to really appreciate it you need to understand mythology. Not really my style. Neither is the book club for that matter, but Maggie said it would be good for me. 'You never know who you might meet,' she said.

***

It's an all-women show except for a solitary man, solitary in more ways than one. Don has a long grey beard and wears socks and sandals all year round, wet season or dry. He sits next to me sometimes and smells of dope and musty sheets that have been stored away for a long time. He rarely speaks, just sits there with a half smile on his face, looking as if he knows something that we all don't. At supper time he piles a huge plateful of whatever is going, and his beard is full of crumbs by the end of the night.

Actually, he did speak to me once. He looked into my eyes and said, 'Have you ever read Proust?'

Not knowing how to respond, I looked down at the carpet and noticed that his big toe was poking through a hole in his sock.

'I think he likes you,' one of the women whispered to me behind her hand.

***

A crack of lightning stirs me from my thoughts. It's only teasing. The build-up has been going on for weeks now. Night after night I sit on this veranda. And still no rain.

The mosquitoes are becoming vicious. I reach for the spray can and douse myself with pungent-smelling repellant. Thunderclaps loudly in the distance, Jim's old blue heeler whimpers at my feet and I pour myself another glass from the cask. The wine makes it easier to breathe the hot heavy air.

One of the neighbours is playing old records. Scratched and squeaky melodies of the sixties come from his window every Friday night. Tonight, he plays 'The Ballad of Easy Rider' over and over.

The cicadas rise to a crescendo. Rain starts to tap on the roof, slowly at first and then gathering pace. Rain – can it really be rain? It taunts you like this sometimes, though – a few drops and then it stops. But no, it keeps coming down hard and fast and splashes at me. The flame of the citronella candle flickers and goes out and I pick up my glass and walk inside.

A huge black moth is plastered to the lounge room wall like a crucifixion figure and the ceiling fan turns with a relentless hum. Alice, asleep on the couch, her face innocent and serene in the amber glow of the table lamp, breathes softly, undisturbed.

Sitting down on the rug beside her, I stare into her sleeping face. I feel my body grow heavy and I lean against the couch, close my eyes, drift.

In a rosy haze I see her, a woman now, laughing and dancing in a field of lilies and butterflies, golden hair flowing down her back, her long white dress clouding around her like smoke.

Thunder rouses me from my reverie and the smell of the rain draws me to the window. The waxy leaves of the tiger lilies shine in the light of the street lamp above – heart-shaped mirrors, waving to me in the wind. I see a face in the fly-spotted window – a middle-aged woman, lined skin and lank silver hair, Medusa-like.

The rain deluges now, like boulders on the roof.

I move away from the window, cover Alice with a sheet, bend down to kiss her cheek and just catch the sweet smell of her breath. I make my way down the hallway to bed.

Centuries later, my heavy eyelids open to see Alice's face looking down at me in the morning light. I reach for a glass of water to quench my burning thirst and to moisten my putrid mouth.

'I dreamt about you last night, Mum,' she says.

'Did you, sweetheart?'

'Yes, Mum. I saw you dancing on your wedding day in a field of lilies. You were lovely, Mum.'

'Oh,' I say, rubbing my eyes. 'How strange. I thought that was my dream.'

I pull on my black silk kimono, the hemline tattered, rotted away by the dank mould-ridden air of six Darwin wet seasons. My kimono was beautiful once.

I switch on the kettle and make a cup of Earl Grey tea. The fragrance of the hot amber liquid stirs my senses awake and I light a stick of incense and push it in a plant pot on the kitchen bench. The scent of sandalwood permeates the kitchen and the smoke wafts upwards in a faint spiral.

A frangipani tree overhangs the veranda. I take my tea out to the veranda and sit under the branches. A blossom – velvet white petals with deep yellow centre – falls at my feet and I reach down for it and put it behind my ear.

Lois is in her driveway, unloading her shopping. She carries a carton of Foster's under one arm and waves to me.

'Not drowning,' I call to her, waving back.

'That's good,' Lois yells over the bougainvillea-laden fence.

The warm sweet tea glides down my throat. Above me in the branches of the frangipani tree, a spider has spun a huge gossamer-like web, seeded with raindrops. Oblivious of me, the black spider is posed dead centre in its own constructed world.

Alice is running around the garden with her friends, laughing loudly and calling, 'I'm a bullseye, I'm a bull'seye.'

For a moment I close my eyes and breathe in the morning air, so fresh now that the wet has finally come.

The insistent ring of the telephone distracts me. I walk barefoot on the floorboards and catch it just before it rings out.

'Hello.'

'This is Don…you know…from the book club.'

'Oh, hello.'

'Would you like to go to a movie tonight?'

'A movie?'

'Yes,' he says, 'a movie.'

'With you?' I say.

'Yes, with me.'

I put the phone down and feeling strangely lighter, I look at myself in the bathroom mirror. I pull my hair into clip and smooth my hands over my face. Somehow the lines don't look so deep this morning; the shadows not so dark. Rummaging in the back of the bathroom cupboard, I pull out an old pumice stone and a bottle of nail varnish, sit down on the edge of the bath and start scrubbing my feet.

Our Darker Purpose

'So, what exactly did happen to the thylacine, Gloria?'

'The Tasmanian tiger? Last I heard, it was extinct. Been extinct since the Great Depression, hasn't it?' she drawled, casually blotting the corners of her mouth with the paper napkin from her latte glass.

A sharp chill was in the breeze that blew from the Derwent that morning. Gusts of wind stirred the litter and lettuce leaves along the gutters of Salamanca Place, and the red, white and green striped market umbrella rattled uncertainly above us. At Gloria's insistence, we sat outside so she could smoke the cigarettes she always carried in her gold cigarette case. She still rolled her own, an ingrained habit from an earlier lifetime, but how elegantly she smoked them now. And not a spot of nicotine on her slim fingers or around the edges of her heart-shaped mouth. Gloria bore no outer stain.

'Cut the crap, Gloria,' I said. 'You know what I mean – the photographs of the animal Dad shot near Zeehan, just before he got sick.'

I'd walked into our father's room just a few days before he died. Gloria was there; Gloria was always there fussing over him and if she wasn't, Raelene was. Asking him where he kept his financial papers, if they could help him with his banking, but never once did I see them cut his toenails or empty his bedpan. The nurse or I would do that. Now his room smelled of illness and death, a smell that even Gloria's perfume could not disguise.

She was down on her knees sorting through his old chest of drawers. 'Dad, you shouldn't leave these photos here. They might be valuable,' Gloria said.

They weren't family photos. No. I saw clearly over her shoulder the colour pictures of our father in a classic Hemingway pose in front of his Range Rover holding the dead beast by its feet. She snatched the bulging yellow Kodak envelope away from me, stuffing it into it into her bag and snapping the clasp firmly shut.

The young dark-haired waiter approached us with a tentative smile. 'More coffee, ladies?'

Gloria smiling seductively said, 'Certainly I do, Charles, but I'm not sure about my older sister here. Claudia? '

'No, thanks,' I muttered. 'The first one was bitter enough. Just a glass of water, please.'

Quietly, almost in a whisper, he looked into my eyes and said, 'Suck my cock.'

'Did you hear what he said to me,' I said.

'What? "Coffee won't be long"?' she replied.

'No. He said… Oh, forget it. The photos, Gloria? Where are they?'

'What would I want with old photos of a dead dog? Claudia, darling, sadly you're imagining things again.'

'And sadly, Gloria, you're a thief. And so is Raelene. It's too cold to sit here any longer, anyway. Gotta catch my bus,' I said, getting up and scraping my chair against the cobble stones.

'Oh, what a shame, Claudia. I was really enjoying our little chat,' said Gloria as she drew deeply on her cigarette. 'Toodles!' she said as she waved her long red index fingernail at me.

I threw two gold coins on the table and walked stiffly into the wind.

Her thin brown tweed coat offered no protection from the biting winter wind; shards of rain stung her face. Reaching Battery Point, she saw a reflection of a crying woman in a shop window. Hair flying, coat flapping, the woman looked deranged. Going to miss the bus if she doesn't hurry. Bus, bus, miss, don't give me that kind of look, miss. Got a screw loose, something missing. Miss mass, a mortal sin, miss! Everybody hates a mismatch, a misfit.

The medication had been helping but there were days when nothing helped; days when the mist hung low over the mountain and ghosts whispered their torments; days like today. Her father had been dead for nearly a year now, but he often seemed so near. Sometimes she woke in the night to see his shade at the end of her bed, staring at her. 'You never loved me like they did, Claudia,' she would hear him say. How they used to fawn all over him; his two beauties, he used to call them.

***

Gloria folded up the brown fur collar of her black cashmere coat, her sleek dark form in sharp relief against the backdrop of the old sandstone buildings. She snapped her mobile phone open and dialled the number with her claws, her brow furrowed.

'Raelene, it's Gloria. Look, I've just had a meeting with the bitch. I've got to talk to you, Sis. I'm coming round. Okay?'

Gloria knocked loudly on the front door.

'Come in, precious. I'll get you a chardy,' said Raelene, kissing the air.

Gloria sat down on Raelene's red leather sofa and lit up a cigarette. 'Don't mind do you, pet?'

'No, of course not. Light one for me.'

Staring out of the window at the view of the Derwent, the sisters sat silently side by side, like animals duplicated in iconography doubling the totemic power. In unison, they sipped from the crystal glasses and smoked their cigarettes. Raelene's hair as dark as Gloria's skin was ivory; they took their beauty completely for granted as the very beautiful always do. Shakespeare understood the power that women, particularly beautiful women, have over men. He understood the seductive power of great beauty.

Gloria drew deeply on her cigarette and raised her glass to Raelene's, 'Our holiday in Greece, darling.'

'What about the solicitor?' said Raelene.

'What about him? Leave him to me.'

***

A small man, looking a little like Winston Churchill without a cigar, the solicitor adjusted his belt around his waist, in the manner that men sometimes have when in the presence of attractive women: an unconscious gesture, you might say. You would think, however, that a solicitor would be more aware of his own body language. Smiling, he beckoned Gloria towards a studded leather chair opposite his massive Huon pine desk.

Sitting down, she crossed her long silky-stockinged legs and ran the tips of her long sinuous fingers across the desk's smooth yellow surface as if tracing for specs of gold dust. 'Beautiful,' she murmured huskily, lowering her head and letting her honey-blonde curls touch it, almost kissing it, then raised her eyes to meet those of the solicitor. She wrapped her elegant hand around his wooden pen holder and luxuriated in its smooth texture, rubbing her hand up and down the length of it. 'Huon as well?' she asked.

'Well, how can I be of service today, Gloria?' he said, rolling his worry beads between his fleshy fingers.

Gloria pulled a white lace handkerchief from her little clutch bag and patted the corners of her eyes. She said she was sorry. She was still very upset about her father's death. It had been a very trying time, as she was sure he could appreciate, she sniffed.

'The death of a parent is always difficult,' said the solicitor.

'Yes, it has been so difficult. Look, I'm not really sure how to put this…' she said, softly, leaning forward and uncrossing and then crossing her legs.

'You can speak to me confidentially, Gloria. You are the executor of the estate, after all,' he said.

'Well,' said Gloria, dabbing her eyes again, 'our sister Claudia has always been, well…highly strung, but now she seems to suffering from delusions about our father and his effects.'

'Delusions?'

'Claudia is claiming that our father shot a thylacine and took a series of photos which prove that it still may exist and that we are keeping them from her. I know how ridiculous that sounds.'

'Claudia did come to see me and I must say I was struck by how… er…unlike you she is. If you don't mind me saying so, you are the most attractive young woman. Some man will be very lucky.'

Gloria ran her fingers through her hair and tipped her head back as if to receive a kiss. 'Claudia says she has voices in her head. It's very sad really. She's on medication.'

No need for Gloria to worry herself any further, the solicitor said. Just let Claudia have copies of any photos. The will was finalised. He would close the file today.

'Thank you for being so kind and understanding. How much did you say?' said Gloria, taking out her cheque book.

***

Scented tea-light candles burning. Cinnamon, I think. Nice in a cake. Fruit cake. Someone called me a fruit cake. Don't like fruit. Rotten. How long have I been coming to her now? Once a week for seven years? Seven years bad luck. How are things? Is your medication helping? Not really. Voices come and go. People always laughing at me. If only I could have been born beautiful like them, someone might have loved me. True beauty shines from within. That's not how the world sees it. Eaten up with jealousy. Is that really how you see yourself? Eaten up with jealousy? Sometimes. Only sometimes? People say I'm paranoid. Always imagining things. Do you think you imagine things? No, No, I don't. Why do you think they exclude you? They are trying to keep things from me. Plotting to keep the photos for themselves. You know, the photos of the Tasmanian tiger that I told you about. I saw those photos. Did he stuff it? Cut its entrails out? Cubs in the pouch? They know all about it. Dogs they are, both of them. But they say I am delusional. Am I? Am I delusional? Cinnamon toast. Yes, sometimes I like cinnamon toast.

'You know, Claudia, I think we might see doctor about increasing your medication. Just for a while anyway, just until this episode passes. All this can be controlled with the correct medication.'

***

Beethoven's Fifth vibrated in my bag and I retrieved the silver messenger from the depths of my worn leather satchel. It is interesting to note that it is a well-known fact that Beethoven was in fact deaf, but he still heard music in his head. It has been argued that he may have suffered from auditory delusions and that he too may have required treatment. I am feeling so much better now that the new medication has kicked in.

'Claudia. This is Gloria. Our father's estate has been finalised at last. Come over and have a drink with us, with Raelene and me and celebrate the end of this silly business.'

It was a long bus ride to Raelene's house. When I arrived, Raelene and Gloria were sitting side by side as usual. They raised their glasses. 'Here's to Dad,' they said together.

'To Dad,' I said.

'We have something for you.' Raelene pushed the box on the coffee table toward me. 'We found it amongst Dad's papers.'

'Go on, darling. Open it,' said Gloria, placing her hand lightly on my knee.

'Oh,' I said. 'Are you sure? Is this some kind of joke?'

'Of course not. You are our sister and Dad's death has been difficult for you. We want you to have it. It might help,' said Gloria, smiling softly into my face.

Carefully, I unfolded the pink tissue paper. Dad's gold fob chain. I had forgotten all about it.

'Put it on,' they both said together.

'I don't know what to say,' I said.

'Here, let me help you with the clasp, darling,' said Gloria, as she came behind me. 'There,' she said. 'It really suits you.'

They both kissed me softly on either side of my face.

'There are no photos of Tasmanian tigers, darling, truly, there aren't. Just family snaps. I've had some copies made for you,' said Gloria.

'We wouldn't keep anything valuable from you, Claudia. You are our sister,' said Raelene.

I felt strangely undeserving and oddly ashamed as the heavy gold fob settled in the hollows of my neck. Perhaps I really didn't know them at all.

'Thank you both, so much. I'll treasure this.'

'Oh yes, and there is a small box of books of Dad's over there in the corner for you. Tasmanian history and stuff. They're of no interest to Gloria and me,' said Raelene, leafing through the Greek travel brochures spread carelessly on the glass coffee table.

'We're always here for you, Claudia. We're your own flesh and blood. Always remember that. Your own flesh and blood,' said Gloria. 'Oh yes. Grab the box of books on your way out, darling.'

Feeling calmer now, the episode seems to have passed, in front of the fire that evening, sorting through the dusty box of books, you remember your father, Larry, as your mother always called him.

You pull out a red-bound book with gold leaf pages: *The Love Poetry of William Shakespeare*. The thinness of the pages feels unlike anything that the father you knew would ever pick up, let alone read; a slim volume of Shakespeare's love sonnets? Your father reading love poems? Perhaps the book was your mother's. You didn't really know your father very well at all, when you face it. How little we ever know anyone, really.

Have you been wrong about your sisters all along? How kind they had been to you earlier. Today, when they sat together, how you wished that you could be part of them: their laughing, their lightness, their beauty. No wonder they avoid you when you accuse them of terrible things. Could things be different? You feel much calmer now with the stronger tablets.

The hypnotic firelight seduces you. You see yourself having coffee with them, sharing in their secrets and looking like them. You imagine another version of yourself – a glamorous worldly you.

Absently, you pick up a Mills & Boon paperback from the bottom of the box. Now that must have been your mother's, surely. You gaze down at the faded cover of the romance: *Love in the Ruins*. You flick rhythmically through the pages as if toying with a pack of Tarot cards. Shuffle the cards well, your mother used to say. Always shuffle the cards well, if you want the truth.

Under the spell of the flames, you see your father take the dead animal from the back of his four-wheel drive parked in our driveway. You watch as, swaggering with the pride of his conquest, he carries the dead beast in one hand by its hind legs and his rifle with the other: the proud hunter returns.

'A beautiful skin but I think I'll stuff it rather than skin it,' he says as he cuts away at his rump steak. He liked it medium rare – the blood running.

'Say no more about it,' you hear your mother say to him. 'Not another word. They'll put you in the slammer for that, Larry. Mark my words. You'll do time if anyone finds out. Just don't ever tell anyone.'

You become aware of the gold fob warm and tight around your neck and recall how your sisters both kissed you softly today. How warm their lips felt. You see the beautiful faces of Gloria and Raelene in the red dancing flames.

The flames flicker. You are jolted from your musings. Softly, without warning, a bunch of sepia negatives fall from your mother's old paperback in a spread on the Axminster.

You pick them up and hold them to the bright firelight.

Gravy and Tragedy

Blowflies buzzed behind the louvres as my mother, Kathleen, fussed over the size eleven chicken that she had stuffed to near bursting with breadcrumbs, onions and sage. Surrounded by mountains of roast potatoes, the pretentious little bird took centre stage on an old plate covered with silver foil. The few precious snow peas that she sent me to pick earlier that morning from over the neighbour's fence she had boiled in mint and sugar. And they were set aside in a small bowl, especially for him.

'Now, Roisin, you stir the gravy in a figure eight shape, like I showed you last time, and put that sprig of rosemary in it and give it a good splash of the tomato sauce,' said she said, little beads of sweat forming on the end of her nose.

She was a long way from Ireland now, my mother, in the hot cramped kitchen in St Kilda, this Christmas Day morning. Humming softly to herself, she patted her swollen belly as she rubbed the small of her back with the palm of her hand. What was it now, that tune she used to hum? 'A Kiss in the Morning, Early'?

'Yes, Mam,' I said, stirring the gravy as I heard my brother and sisters laughing joyously in the backyard.

'Send it higher,' yelled Pat (always the boss of the games).

We all got a yo-yo each – mine was still in my apron pocket. The peals of laughter coming through the backdoor gave me hope that, maybe, everything would be all right. But the storm clouds were gathering – I had a sense for it in those days.

Stealing a sideways glance to the lounge room, I saw the back of my father's head. Smoking a cigarette, he sat silently next to the tinsel-laden Christmas tree; beside him was a near-empty bottle of whiskey.

The fragrant rosemary wafted from the thick brown sauce that began to stiffen and bubble in the cast-iron pan, the lava-like liquid rising and falling, little volcanoes, releasing steam, simmering and hissing at me. Something tightened in my stomach. I looked again at the back of my father's head, his small ears tight against his sleek, oiled black hair as he poured the last of the whiskey into the glass. With the old cracked wooden spoon I kept stirring: figure eight, figure eight and figure eight….

'Get that gravy off now, Roisin,' my mother yelled at me. 'You're boiling the life out of it, girl.'

Pouring the dark liquid into a large white gravy boat with a fine gold line around the rim, she wiped the lip carefully with a thin tea towel and placed it gently on the matching saucer. 'There,' she said with pride. Elegant and swan-like in shape, it was the only piece of finery on my mother's dresser. A wedding present from her own mother in Ireland, this graceful vessel demanded reverence. I ran my fingertips lightly over the smooth, curved porcelain sides, feeling its fineness. Once, when a neighbour had visited, I heard her say, 'It's Royal Doulton, you know. Royal Doulton.'

'Stop fiddling now, and go and put that on the table,' she said. 'And call your brother and sisters for their Christmas dinner.'

Earlier, Bridget, Mary and I had set the red laminex table with our mother's only white damask tablecloth, smoothed the creases out and made sure that the stain from last year was not at the head of the table. We had made a centrepiece from votive candles, tinsel and old pine cones and I had scratched my hand on the holly.

Stealing past my silent father, I placed the steaming gravy next to the chicken that sat at the head of the table, ready for him to carve. The little ones and Pat ran in from outside, pulling their chairs out noisily, all eagerness to sit down, and excitedly took their places at the table, the light from the candles reflecting in their eyes. Faces of our dead grandparents stared down at us from the dresser – faded sepia images accepting an unspoken invitation. Next to them was an old photograph of our father as he once had been, a brave fresh-faced boy, off to the war to return a hero, or so he had been told.

'Now, you all be behaving yourselves or there'll be no Christmas pudding for ye,' our mother said. 'Roisin, go call your father to the table.'

Smelling the whiskey as I stood next to his chair, I said, just above a whisper, 'Dad, Christmas dinner is ready.'

'Christmas dinner, by Jove, is it?' he said, standing and swaying a little. 'Get out of my way, you,' he said, and I jumped nervously aside. He walked slowly and deliberately to the table, picked up the carving knife and fork and started to carve the chicken.

'Frank, we haven't said grace yet,' said our mother.

'No,' our father replied quietly, 'we haven't said grace yet.'

He continued carving the chicken roughly, the meat coming off in chunks, and then savagely, until the ribcage was exposed. A piece of the greasy skin hit me in the face.

'Look at this half-starved bloody pigeon. Look at it, would you! It wouldn't feed a feckin' cat. Is this the best you could do, Kathleen?' he yelled, his eyes burning.

'Frank, I did some snow peas especially for ye,' our mother's soft voice faltered.

All trace of laughter and talk had disappeared from the table as we all sat there motionless, watching as our father mutilated the pitiful chicken. The Christmas chicken was now an irreverent pile of flesh and skin, the bread seasoning scattered in hunks on the table.

Plunging the fork in, he pulled up the chicken's anus and held it high in the air. 'Now, who is going to be the lucky one – who is going to eat the parson's nose?'

Smiling at Pat, he reached over and threw it on his plate. Our hero Pat – our brave laughing brother, the boss of the games – his face turned pale. My stomach knotted. I knew what is coming. The horrible thing sat on Pat's plate with its greasy tendrils and veins poking out, a hideous fatty lump of goosebump flesh.

'Eat it,' our father said menacingly, standing above us all. 'Nobody's moving till you eat it.'

Pat, white-faced, tears trickling down his cheeks, picked up his knife and fork and poked bravely at the anal flesh. I felt his throat constricting.

'Frank, it's Christmas. Please,' pleaded our mother.

'Christmas, is it?' His face contorted as he reached in front of me and belted Pat hard across the head, smashing his face into his plate. 'Leave the table, you snivelling brat, if you can't eat the Christmas dinner that your mother has cooked for you. Get out, get out,' he yelled, his face red and senseless with rage.

Pat jumped from the table and ran out the back door, holding his head down, blind with pain and humiliation. In the breath of Pat's departure, the rest of us just sat there, frozen in fear for endless seconds. And then our father, he picked up our mother's gravy boat.

'Oh, Mother of God,' gasped Kathleen.

He hurled the precious gravy boat against the picture of the Sacred Heart that hung tragically on our kitchen wall. The fine porcelain shattered and flew through the air as our father collapsed heavily in the chair at the end of the table, his great broad shoulders heaving with harsh, rasping, broken sobs.

***

Later, when my father was safely snoring in his armchair and the whiskey all gone, I went up behind the garden shed, the late afternoon air heavy now with honeysuckle and the lingering traces of the neighbourhood's day of cooking. And there was Pat, as I knew he would be, alone in the corner. It was where he always went – in the corner where the old shed meets the ivy-covered brick wall. Alone, crouched, cowering, ashamed of his hot tears, and yet but ten years old, he was unmoving as I sat next to him.

'I've brought you some Christmas pudding – it's got a sixpence in it,' I said.

He didn't answer. He kept his head down on his knees, the shame of the tears too much.

'I won't tell the others,' I said.

Bridget and Mary had started playing. I could hear their soft little girl's laughter as they started up again with their yo-yo tricks.

'Where's Pat? Pat, Pat!' they called timidly.

He rose slowly, looking at me now with his boy's face shadowed by a bruise that had marked his soul. He pulled the sixpence out of the pudding and put it in his pocket. To me he said, 'Here, hold me pud for us, would ya,' and ran off to join his sisters. 'I'm coming,' he called.

They started playing again, tentatively, gently, like sunshine after rain. The familiar noise of our mother washing the dishes clattered through the kitchen louvres and the wireless crackled the strains of 'White Christmas' in the late afternoon breeze.

Eulogy For a Myth

There is a place in the artist's heart where all things are bearable, no matter how terrible, where experience is sifted through, consecrated, hallowed and transformed into something we call art.

The soft purring of the telephone woke Rosa from a deep, middle-of-the-night sleep.

It was her sister Sophia with the news. 'Five minutes ago. The nurse has turned everything off. He's gone…at last.'

Although it was a summer's night, Rosa pulled the doona tightly around her thin body and sat on the edge of the bed, unmoving until dawn. Above her bed hung a gold-framed print of Leda and the Swan, mirroring her pose. The early morning light was harsh and bright and the singing of the birds seemed bleakly incongruous on this, the morning after her father's death.

The sun was high in the sky when the phone rang again. The funeral was arranged for Friday, Sophia said, and of course Rosa was expected to be there. She was expected to read the eulogy as she had promised. Her brothers would be there and Nick was making sure that it was going to be a big occasion, a day to remember, a day to honour their father. 'You have to be there, Rosa. Don't worry about Nick and Spyros,' said Sophia.

Strange how the writing the eulogy had taken on such significance. She felt pressed to finish it even though he had still been alive and now, for some elusive reason, she felt a burning urge to read her piece. Glancing in the dressing table mirror, she looked at her pale, drawn face and smoothed her thick unruly hair. I've got his hair, she thought. I've always had his hair. Rosa began packing her suitcase.

At the airport, the two sisters hugged. They drove home through the dark suburban streets, detouring past their father's house, now unlit but tomorrow they would all be there for the wake. The family home, a neo-classic mansion in the heart of suburbia, with its pillared portico was like a cenotaph for all that her father held to be important in the world, a memento mori of a kind.

Rosa remembered how the aroma of her father's cigars and the expensive smell of the perfume mingled in the summer night air, especially after he committed her mother to a nursing home. Rosa detested the smell of cigars, still.

'Are you up for a few drinks?' said Rosa.

'Not too many. Nick and Spyros are picking us up at nine o'clock for the viewing.'

'Viewing?'

'A private viewing of the body. Dad's body, at the funeral parlour,' said Sophia.

Morning came again, as mornings do, but this particular morning had a sharpness; everything seemed clearer, the colours more intense than usual.

Loud knocking on the front door made Rosa jump, her hot black coffee splashing on the carpet as Sophia opened the door to her two suit-clad brothers, Nick and Spyros. They look like undertakers, thought Rosa. Two bloody undertakers! Nick had slicked his hair back into a ponytail and Spyros had done the same. Spyros, who had always been several inches smaller than Nick, looked like a carbon copy of his older brother, only smaller and rounder.

Nick walked toward Rosa, still talking on his mobile phone, his expensive aftershave filling the room. She winced at his approach, but he smiled at her with his perfectly capped teeth, and Spyros nodded to her. Relieved, she smiled back.

Finishing his call, Nick unbuttoned his jacket and sat down next to her. 'Glad you could make it, Rosa,' he said. 'You going to say some nice words about the old man, huh? Let everyone know what he was like?'

'Yes, Nick.'

'I never was much good with words. Just make sure you get it right, Rosa,' he said, smiling at her again and dusting a stray hair off his shoulder. 'Like the suit? Italian wool.'

She thought how much he looked like their father and how little like their mother he was. Mama had waited on the boys as if they had been little gods, but she used to cry to the Virgin Mary and pound her breast with her fist, mea maxima culpa, when she heard the sound of the leather strap her husband used to 'make men of them, to make them ready for the world'. Sophia had tried to tell Mama that her husband had died but all she did was laugh and ask what time the boys would be home from school.

Rosa felt a little more relaxed now. Nick had smiled at her; he had forgiven her and that meant Spyros had forgiven her. She hadn't seen either of them for over a year; not since the terrible argument she had had with her father.

'You apologise to the old boy, bitch,' Nick had said. 'You hear me, bitch. You hear me,' as he stabbed her in the chest with his finger. 'The old boy's sick. The past is the past. Leave it there.'

'Yeah, you apologise, bitch, ya hear,' echoed Spyros.

Rosa never apologised.

Nick's phone rang.

'Business waits for no man,' he said smiling at her, again. He had a way of leaning forward when he spoke on his phone, holding it to his ear almost lovingly, his voice taking on a kind of religious intensity.

'Got the little bastard. The old man would have been happy about that,' said Nick as he snapped his phone shut. 'Okay, girls. Spyros. Youse ready? Let's go see the old man. This is his big day.'

Nick held the door open for Sophia and Rosa when they arrived at the funeral chapel. The funeral was at midday; the drive to the church was slow. The air inside the church was heavy with the heat of cramped bodies on the hot January afternoon. Familiar faces of their father's family and friends – old women wearing black dresses and gold jewellery, dabbing their eyes with white handkerchiefs, pot-bellied men in suits, their hands clasped respectfully in front of them – nodded to them and smiled as Rosa, Sophia, Nick and Spyros made their way their family pew. Their father's coffin was blanketed in a thick cover of red roses.

Silence fell and shuffling ceased as the priest began. He spoke quietly, comfortingly. What a well-loved and respected man their father was. Hadn't he always been there to help his friends and hadn't he shown outstanding love for his family?

When it was time, the priest motioned Rosa to the pulpit. She watched herself as she stood in front of the large congregation and heard herself read without flinching, except for a brief pause when she noticed that she had made a spelling error.

'Our father began his life in this town and ended it here, but the road he walked was often a difficult one. He started his life with a market stall and ended it as a director of a company. Nothing stood in his way… He met his foes bravely and slayed his dragons boldly. In the end he met death with dignity and courage. A great poet once said, "Cowards die many times before their death, the valiant never taste death but once." We love you, Dad, we thank you and wish a safe journey home.'

At the wake, the funeral attendants now seemed to have metamorphosed into waiters passing around smoked salmon and drinks on silver trays. The ouzo was warm against her throat and the late afternoon was paling to a dull grey. It was over now. He was laid to rest and she would be returning on a plane home tomorrow, back to her life.

'That was a good reading you did, Rosa. You was always good with words. Me, I was always good with figures…and making money, like the old man,' Nick laughed a hollow laugh and put his arm around Rosa, hugging her. 'You finished your novel yet?'

'Yeah,' said Spyros. 'That was a good story you told about the old man, Rosa.'

'The old man would have liked it. He would have been proud. The only writing I'm good at is writing cheques. Get it, Rosa. – writing cheques!' said Nick, laughing loudly at his own joke.

Spyros looked at Nick. 'You get that deal before, Nick? Is the bastard going to sign tonight?'

'Yeah, Spyros. I snapped him, mate. The lawyer rang before. He signed already.'

Her father's favourite music played softly in the background – 'Zorba's Dance'. Rosa remembered how he used to love to dance to it at his parties with his friends, over and over till they collapsed. Someone had turned the music up and Nick and Spyros had their arms around each other now, dancing and laughing, tossing their undertakers' jackets high in the air and passing the ouzo bottle one to the other. The music got louder and faster and they danced and laughed until they fell down together on the grass, wiping the tears of laughter from their faces.

'Hey, Nick,' said Spyros, trying to control his choking laughter, 'remember the night the old man belted you nearly fuckin' senseless when you lost him that deal. You was about sixteen. Remember, remember that, Nick. Mate, I thought that he was going to fuckin' kill you.' Spyros punched Nick in the shoulder, 'Remember that, mate.'

Nick covered his face with his hands and sank to his knees. He let out a low moan and then a deep rasping sound like a branch cracking from a tree trunk.

The day drew to night. The family gathered close together, seeking comfort from the presence of the bloodline, looking into each other's faces for meaning. Somehow Rosa knew that this closeness was ephemeral and would pass as the pain of their father's death faded.

For Rosa, the next day, the journey homeward was cold and long. Her flat felt strangely empty when she walked in. The loneliness started to settle on her. Tired after her trip, she didn't feel like going out. Too unsettled and restless for writing. Something – what was it? Imagination playing tricks? The night was warm; she sat in a cane chair on the veranda and let her mind drift.

Proud to be with her father, handsome in his navy-blue jacket, she had worn her pink party dress that morning. Edgy, he was going to do a business deal. Hadn't made a sale in months, things were closing in, unopened bills on the mantelpiece piled high. The bank was ready to foreclose. He had to clinch this deal. Everything depended on it.

Her father held her tightly by her wrist and led her down the hotel corridor. The man who answered the door was dark, pot-bellied and smelled of lavender water, his black hair oiled to his head and neck. Rosa remembered watching with the fascination of innocence the beads of sweat forming on her father's brow.

The two men spoke in quietly and her father still held her by her wrist. The man scratched his belly, smiled a gold-toothed smile and looked down at her. She shivered as he stroked her cheek and wrapped his hot hand around her thin neck.

'Let me think about it. Leave the little girl with me for a while,' he said. 'Leave the little girl with me. Come back in an hour and I'll let ya know,' the man said, taking hold of Rosa's plaits with his big fleshy paw.

She stared at her father's back as he walked down the passage. 'Dad… Dad.'

But he didn't turn back.

Making up stories in her head, telling lies, just like Nick always said she did. 'You analyse stuff too much, Rosa, you and your arty farty friends. Making mountains out of bugger all. Shit just happens.'

She moved around her flat, flicking the television, glossing through a magazine. She thought back to the funeral and to the consoling words of her father's friends, 'Your father was such a good man, loved what you wrote about him, so lucky to have such a fine father.'

Why did she think these things? Pacing. Ring the counsellor tomorrow; she said to contact her any time; she said it could be difficult. Sleep always helps, she thought. Block it out for now. Lying on her bed, she closed her eyes.

The dream came again. A painting, large sunset, Dali-like, crimson glow, darkening, trees, dark face, her father's face. His expression? Kind, smiling? No. Not kind – harsh face. Heart pounds. Repaint the picture: frantic brush strokes. Paint won't stay. The more she paints, the more the paint drips off the canvas. Frantic brush strokes. Canvas a mirror now. Little girl with black plaits comes through the mirror, reaches out and takes her hand and smears it with paint.

Rosa woke wiping the paint from her hands. Oh yes, a dream. Vaguely she thought someone was smoking a cigar and drifted back to sleep. But in the morning, the coffee tasted good. She felt energised, light as if she had slept for a year. From her wardrobe she chose a bright red shirt and sprayed herself with French perfume.

As a girl, Rosa had made altars to the Blessed Virgin but the altars of her adulthood were different than those of her girlhood. Now she burnt incense and oils and made prayers and offerings of all kinds. She had made one on the morning her father died and the pears that she had piled in a bowl in front of a statue of the goddess of the green Tara had started to rot. The smell of the over-ripe fruit was strong.

The devil telephone rang to disturb her from her reverie.

It was Sophia. 'I'm coming to Melbourne for the weekend. Put me up tonight, okay?'

Rosa was laying the table when Sophia arrived. Rosa lit a candle and they ate, drank and talked, mainly gossip about friends.

'Nothing quite like the light relief of the odd bit of scandal, is there?' Rosa said.

She looked at Sophia's dark brown eyes, heavy brows, his eyes. Sophia got his eyes. Their small talk lulled.

'Rosa,' said Sophia, pouring herself another large goblet of red and topping up Rosa's drink, 'did you really mean all that stuff you said about Dad?'

'I'm not sure what you're talking about.'

'You know, all that stuff you said about Dad in the eulogy. You know, about him being such a hero and all.'

'Why do you ask?' said Rosa, her voice taking on an edge.

Sophia took a deep sip of her wine. 'Well, let's face it, Rosa. You didn't get on all that well with him, did you?'

'We had our moments,' said Rosa.

'Had your moments all right. You hated the poor old fella, didn't you, Rosa? And after all he'd given you, all he'd done for you.'

The candle Rosa had lit earlier had long since burned out and was now a waxy heap on the saucer. Sophia took another long sip of her wine and filled her goblet again.

'I don't know what you mean,' said Rosa.

'Crap, you don't know what I mean. You know exactly what I mean. What was all that poetry stuff? "Cowards die many times" or some crap. It wasn't even your line – Shakespeare said that. Julius bloody Caesar, wasn't it?'

Sophia stood up and walked towards the little altar. 'Praying to goddesses now, Rosa? Don't think they're going to help you. Face it, Rosa. You hated the old boy. You said terrible things about him before he died.'

'But the value is in the myth,' blurted Rosa.

'What fucking value is "in the myth"? You writers are all the fucking same. At the funeral, you were just there taking notes for your next story, weren't you, Rosa? You weren't even there. You weren't really at your father's funeral – you were up in the bloody clouds somewhere writing your myths. You writers steal from life and turn it into your so-called art!' yelled Sophia.

Rosa sank lower in her chair and bowed her head into her hands. Her voice muffled now, she said almost inaudibly, 'I need the myth more than I need the truth.'

When Rosa got up the next morning, Sophia was gone. She had left a note on the altar. Scrawled in a rough hand it read:

Dear Rosa,

If you want to know why I've gone, why don't you consult the oracle and write another fucking story about it? Write another myth. Write another lie.

Sophia

Rosa lit another candle, held the note above the flame and the ashes fell like petals. Sitting down at the desk, she started to write, humming softly to the tune of 'Zorba's Dance'.

Verification

It was white chocolate, definitely white, of that I am sure.

The painting my father had brought to the art dealer's house was a watercolour. This man was an expert. He was going to tell my father if it was a Turner or not. If it was a Turner, the art dealer would buy it, and my father could pay all the bills that were piling up, unopened behind the clock on our mantelpiece. My father had taken me along for company, hadn't he?

The house was big and dark and smelled the same as the chocolate. The chocolate had that musty smell, as though it had been opened and left sitting untouched in its wrapper for too long. It was broken into uneven pieces with edges ragged and sharp. He offered it to me on a plate, a white plate – chipped, I think. His hands were the hands of an old man, the backs of them shiny and speckled with brown spots. His fingers were bent and wrinkly, fingernails yellow and long. Needed cutting. Mum always cut my fingernails. Usually in the bath.

Would you like a piece? Yes, please, trying so hard to be good. Trying so hard to be polite and thinking of Mum cutting my fingernails in the bath. Leave the little girl with men for a while, he said. Leave her with me.

My father's back was stiff as he walked away, down the hallway, out the front door. The chocolate was hard and stale. It tasted like it smelled – musty. The man's breath was sour and his hands were dry and hard. Did I like school? Yes. Was I good girl? Yes? Could I keep a secret?

Where did my father go? Did he sit in the car and smoke Capstan unfiltered cigarettes? Did he bite his nails? Or did he read the paper and drink a cup of tea from a polystyrene cup?

On the way home, my father stopped at a garage and bought me an album for cards with pictures of butterflies, or was it free with the petrol? I was sent to bed early that night. I collected the butterfly cards for years after that. My mother was pleased the man had bought the painting.

It was definitely white chocolate. White chocolate, on a plate.

Venus

Lara looked out of the bedroom window across to the dam surrounded by wattle trees which blazed brilliant yellow in the morning sum. Another wild orchid might bloom today, she thought. Reaching for her silk kimono, she began to put it on but, changing her mind, she let it slide over her naked body and drop to the floor. She turned and stood for a moment, watching her husband as he slept. He was snoring softly. He rolled over on to his side and yawned.

As she began walking to the door, she heard him whisper behind her, 'Venus.'

Lara smiled, not looking behind her, not wanting him to see she was pleased. Yes, Jim really did love her, she thought. In the kitchen she made Orange Pekoe tea and croissants, all the while enjoying the sensation of wearing only the strand of Japanese pearls that Jim had given her for their last anniversary.

She carried the tray back to the bedroom. Feeling chilled now, she slipped her kimono over her shoulders, luxuriating in the feel of the soft silk against her body, the faint smell of rose oil from last night's bath lingering.

Sitting down at her dressing table, she twisted her long, dark hair into a loose knot. She dabbed Chanel Number 5 on her nipples and dipped her finger into a little pot of honey-coloured gloss and dabbed it across her wide mouth.

She gazed at herself in the mirror. She found herself yearning to feel love for a man again the way she used to love Jim; her feelings for him had changed with the passing of the years. But he loved her still. For now, that would have to be enough.

She walked across and touched the familiar cheek with the back of her hand.

They'd arranged to meet their friends that afternoon at their favourite café. They browsed the tightly packed bookshelves while they were waiting for Peter and Maria to arrive.

'They didn't have a sexual relationship, you know,' said Lara, leafing through a book.

'Who didn't?' Jim said absently, reaching in front of her for a biography of Winston Churchill.

'Heathcliff and Cathy.'

'Well, if they didn't, Heathcliff did an awful lot of wandering the moors and bashing his head against trees for a man who hadn't even got his leg over,' said Jim.

'Not everything is about sex, you know,' she said, smiling, remembering the morning they had just spent together.

'So, are you going to buy yet another copy of Wuthering Heights?' said Jim.

'Yes. Nice hardbacks of the old classics are hard to find.'

'There they are,' said Jim calling to their old friends and pointing to the courtyard outside. 'Nice day to sit in the sun,' he said.

Peter looked dapper in his straw boater and Maria looked like she had 'made an effort'. She was wearing a blue and red floral shirt, white beads and white linen pants. Lara noticed that Maria had sat on something – maybe a plum – but she decided not say anything. You could still be 'cool' in middle age, whatever the kids might think – nonchalance was still a great pose. Lara tried it as often as she could.

Greetings over, Peter said, 'That one over there by the lavender bush okay?'

The day was glorious summer and Lara wore a cream linen wrap skirt with a white sleeveless shirt that showed off her tan. The solarium sessions had paid off and the bronzed effect made her feel healthy and just a little superior to those with freckled white bodies. She pinched her hips and thought wryly that the days were gone when she could feel her hipbones. Each passing year she promised herself that she would diet. But Jim had called her Venus this morning, hadn't he? He'd always said how he loved her breasts, which were still round and firm. He said they sat perfectly in the palms of his hands. Lara felt the sun burning her shoulder and moved closer under the umbrella and was pleased as she brushed against Maria's hip, feeling it to be more ample than her own.

'What's this, Lara?' asked Peter, picking up Wuthering Heights. 'Don't tell me you like this melodrama. Heathcliff and Cathy – what a hopeless pair of co-dependents they were.'

'A typical psychologist's response,' said Lara, smiling.

'Not a romantic bone in his body. Take no notice of him, Lara,' laughed Maria.

Peter put his arm around Maria and kissed her cheek. 'You still love me, though.'

She kissed him back.

'Don't mind if I smoke, do you?' He lit up, and the aroma of the cigarette and the hat gave him the air of a gangster.

'He's never going to be able to quit,' said Maria, waving her hands in mock despair.

Maria's hands had that podgy looks that comes from wearing too many rings in sizes way too small for short plump fingers. Lara was grateful that her hands still looked good. She had a French manicure every week.

The waiter approached them.

'Hang the coffee,' said Jim. 'I'll have a glass of red. It's Sunday.'

'Same,' said Peter. 'Champagne, girls?'

The waiter set their drinks down and Peter lit up again.

'So long, Marianne' droned on in the background.

'Leonard Cohen,' said Jim.

Lara sipped her champagne.

Maria giggled, saying, 'I love the feeling of the bubbles going up your nose.'

Peter patted her knee.

'Australia did well in the cricket,' said Peter.

'Oh…yes,' said Jim, oddly distracted.

A young woman was approaching the table. She would have been about twenty-five and smelled strongly of sandalwood. Stopping squarely in front of Jim, she smiled at him, her pearly teeth perfectly even. Blonde hair brushed her shoulders; her unmade-up face was clear and pretty. Her silver jewellery sparkled in the sun and her white muslin dress fell softly against the curves of her young body.

'Oh…Venus… What a surprise.'

'Hello, Jim. I'm meeting a friend. Love it here. Great books and wonderful coffee, don't you think? Can see you're busy. Talk to you soon.' Tossing her soft fair hair over her shoulder, she glided gracefully away, like a swan on a lake.

'Well, Jim. You're a dark horse, old son. Who was that gorgeous creature?'

'Err…just a student…has a passion for the Romantic poets. Been helping her with a project.'

'Bet you have,' joked Peter, digging him in the ribs. 'Passion for the Romantics, eh.'

'Men,' said Maria. 'What can you do with them?'

Lara watched Jim as his eyes followed the girl as she seemed to float her way to the table opposite. He was transfixed, as if transported to another world. Something stirred in Lara, a memory, recognition. Jim's look – hunger, yearning, adoration? She'd forgotten until now that he used to look at her like that. When was the last time? She didn't know it was the last time? We never know if something is for the last time, she thought.

The young woman's boyfriend arrived, his polo collar turned up against his neck and wearing a musky scent that smelled like sex. 'Hi, babe,' he said, sitting opposite her. He was blond like her, but as tall and muscular as she was small and delicate.

He reached across and took her hand in his and they sat staring into each other's eyes. The girl laughed delicately and he kissed the inside of her wrist. A leaf fell in her hair and he reached over and took it, kissed it and put it in his pocket.

'Who was that old guy you were talking to?' he asked.

'Oh, nobody much. Just a lecturer at uni – bit of an old fart really,' she said, trying to keep her voice low, but not low enough.

Jim's shoulders slowly dropped. His face seemed suddenly lined and his thinning scalp glistened with sweat under the summer sun and his cheeks flushed from the wine. Now, he looked like a version of his own father. His smile faded.

Lara fixed a smile on her face and continued to talk to Peter and Maria, but the words fell like pebbles from her mouth. Jim was silent. The mournful tones of Leonard Cohen droned on in the background. The sun went behind a cloud.

***

'Don't think I'll watch TV tonight, Lara. Too tired. Touch of the sun,' said Jim.

'What about the casserole? It's nearly ready,' said Lara.

Jim seemed vague, preoccupied. He looked his sixty years tonight.

'Night,' she called after him as he slunk down the passage.

Lara turned on the television. She felt small and alone on the three-seater couch. The clock ticked loudly, so she turned up the sound, unaware of the program. The smell of the casserole cooking made her sad and nauseous simultaneously. She walked around the house turning off the lights, took the casserole out of the oven and sat it on the bench, untouched.

At school, she remembered the English teacher had asked the class what they thought was more important – to love or be loved. Lara couldn't remember her answer, but she knew now. 'Life will teach you,' the teacher had said. 'Life will teach you.'

She padded barefoot down the passage and put on the kimono she had worn that morning. Under the fluorescent bathroom light, it had lost its lustrous pearl sheen, looked dull and had a dark coffee stain on the front. It smelled musty and felt slightly damp. Leaning closer to the bathroom mirror, she saw a new crop of grey hairs at her temple and her eyebrows looked overgrown and bushy. She looked down and noticed the varicose vein in her leg seemed more raised and blue than usual.

Unable to bear the night alone any longer, she got into bed next to Jim, curled into the foetal position and leaned against his back. He snored loudly. Lara remembered when she and Jim had first met, she used to call him Heathcliff and he would laugh and kiss her. She remembered the first time they argued, that he had cried. She thought of the twelve red roses he had given her on their first anniversary and how he bashful he had looked when he pulled them from behind his back.

She felt cold even though it was a warm summer's night. Lara dozed fitfully. Odd dreams came and went like visitations. She dreamt she was a girl again playing with a hula hoop; she dreamt Jim had sung her the song that he had written for her years ago.

Sometime just before dawn, in that very silent hour before the first bird sings, she awoke. Lara lay waiting for the comfort of the first bird song, the promise of a new day.

Then in the stillness she heard Jim sobbing in his sleep, quietly at first and then muffled, 'Venus,' and then loudly, 'Venus…my love…my beautiful love,' he cried. His cries trailed back into sleep and he began to snore again.

Like a woman sleepwalking, Lara got out of bed and went to the hall cupboard. It creaked loudly, like a scream in the dark when she opened it. Reaching in, she pulled out a suitcase. She left a note under an apple on the kitchen bench.

Jim woke to the early morning sunlight reaching to the empty side of the bed. Thinking of tea and croissants, he rolled over and stole a few extra minutes' sleep. Waking for the second time, he felt chilled now that the early sun had dulled. Reaching over, he pulled back the drapes seeing a grey day.

'Lara,' he called expectantly. Feeling slightly annoyed, scratching his head, he made his way to the kitchen stubbing his toe on the way. His worn underpants hung loosely around his hips. Lara had threatened so many times to throw them out.

He saw the untouched casserole on the bench, lifted the lid. A beef number – would be nice with a bottle of red for the two of them tonight, he thought. He crossed his arms in front of him, rubbing his shoulders, feeling cold in the unheated kitchen. Funny, usually Lara had the kettle on by the time he got up.

Absently he took a bite from an apple and picked up the note. He sank slowly to the kitchen stool, and felt his mouth go dry. He read the note again and then again.

'Venus,' he said softly, his voice breaking, 'my love.'

La Tristesse…

Vincent Van Gogh's Still Life: Vase with Fifteen Sunflowers hung on the wall of the solicitor's waiting room, the same print that had hung above the king-sized bed in the honeymoon suite where her marriage had begun fifteen years ago. Then it had seemed to her a cheerful scene – a bunch of yellow flowers in a vase.

The tortuous yellow flowers had borne silent witness to their clumsy lovemaking in those early hopeful days and it seemed almost prophetic to her that the picture should re-appear in her life at this moment. Fifteen flowers. Each flower so different, contorted and misshapen in an expression of discrete anguish, yet together the flowers formed a perfect composition. She stared at the picture and thought how each wretched flower could be a representation of each year of her marriage – a composition most imperfect.

The sunflowers are ravaged, she thought. You can almost hear them screaming their agonies. She remembered learning at school how Van Gogh had loved yellow, how he saw it as a symbol of light both within and without the human heart. But his sunflowers are not really yellow, she thought – more mustard, variations of many different shades of mustard – such a cold and piteous colour.

She thought back to her schooldays and her sophisticated French teacher, Madame Gachet, a little woman with bobbed black hair, painted red lips who always smelled heavily of Chanel Number 5. Madame had travelled the world and had visited the Van Gogh museum in Amsterdam. She spoke often of the sunflower paintings and Van Gogh. 'Such a tragic man,' she would say. 'Tragic, yet wonderful.'

'*La tristesse durera toujours.*' Vincent uttered those words just before he died, Madame had told the told the class one day.

She remembered how Madame Gachet asked her to write the English translation on the blackboard and she how scrawled slowly in her schoolgirl's hand, 'The sadness will last forever.'

She stared again at the Sunflowers. How he must have suffered as a man and as an artist, she thought. What was it that finally caused him to end it? Was it one specific event that made him succumb to despair? Or was it a series of events, like the contorted projections expressed in his Sunflowers, events that pressed so heavily in on him that he could bear the world no longer and he took a gun to his chest?

Don't think of these things now, she told herself. Think of something else. She watched the couple sitting opposite, their heads down discussing what she could see was an old handwritten cash book. Could they be mother and son? Yes, that would seem most likely – the man looked much younger than the woman, who was telling him that she had trusted 'Dad' but now she realised that she had been foolish to do so.

Why did 'Dad' leave? Another woman? Younger? Prettier? Men are all the same. It would have been another woman. There is always another woman.

'Thousands are missing,' the woman said, pointing to the leather-bound book, and the young man was shaking his head. Perhaps it would mean less inheritance for him.

Ah, it's not good to be so cynical but life can have that effect on a person after a while. She smoothed her skirt with her sweaty palms. Calm down, she told herself, and reached for a glossy magazine on the glass table in front of her. Turning the pages distractedly, she tried to arrange her thoughts.

The family law specialist stepped out of his office and walked toward her, his hand outstretched, 'Anna. I'm sorry to have kept you waiting. Come in.' He held the door open for her and looked her up and down from behind before she sat down. 'What can I do for you?'

'Just the cold hard facts, thanks.'

'Okay. How long have you been married?'

'Fifteen years.'

'Children?'

'Our son. He's fourteen.'

'Property?'

'Our home. An average family home. Brick. Three bedrooms. And two cars.'

'Domestic violence?'

'No, only emotional violence.'

'Ah, yes. Happy families all are alike but unhappy families are unhappy in their own way. Or something like that. Who said that? Tolstoy, wasn't it?' said the lawyer.

He wore a long pink silk tie and, as he questioned her, she noticed that he had the habit of waving the end of it up and down as he spoke. I wonder what his wife is like, she thought.

'My husband doesn't want to end the marriage. He has refused, in fact. It's not because of any great love or affection for me – he just doesn't want to split his assets and risk not seeing as much of his son. He's probably got a girlfriend, for all I know. I'm sure he has. We don't have sex with me any more – he doesn't even look at me unless he has to. I can't even remember the last time he kissed me.'

She thought of the phone calls late at night that he took downstairs when he thought she was asleep, the faint smell of perfume on his jacket and how occasionally he slipped and called her by her name – Michelle. What are you like, Michelle? Are you blonde and clear-skinned? Do you look like I used to look? Do you laugh like I used to laugh? Does he kiss you on the inside of your thigh? Has he told you that he will love always?

'And you? Have you got anyone else?'

'There was someone for a while…but it didn't work out. He was married with kids… I was years older than he was,' she said.

She sighed as she thought of Victor, and felt the tears well up. Her friends had said that she had an obsession for him and that she needed help. What did they know of obsession? What did they know of love for that matter, in their boring little lives, with their pay television, Sunday barbecues and husbands in suits?

Obsession. She liked the word. Yes, maybe she had been obsessed, but she loved Victor more than she had ever loved anyone. And still she loved him; still she yearned for him. She thought of him now, his soft blue eyes, fine blond hair and brown surfer's face. How she had begged him not to end it. Oh, Victor. She thought of the night when they had lit a fire on the beach and had watched the sun go down.

The lawyer was waving the end of his long pink silk tie backwards and forwards. 'So, you want the cold hard facts. Well, it's like this. If your husband doesn't want to end the marriage and he plays hardball, it's going to be tough for you. You'd probably have a hard time convincing a fourteen-year-old boy to leave his home, his friends and his father. You would have to be the one to leave. It doesn't sound like that would worry your husband much. If you leave and your son won't go with you, you'll lose him and the house and you'll be lucky if you end up with enough money for a unit somewhere.' He continued waving the end of his pink tie.

'So, things haven't changed that much since *Anna Karenina*?' she said.

'Your namesake, Anna.'

'What I meant was that it is not that easy to get out of a marriage if you have a child.'

'Yes. In fact, divorce is the easy bit. It's just paperwork. It's the bit in between marriage and divorce that's hard.'

He sees women like me everyday, Anna thought. He probably thinks that I'm just another middle-aged woman who's left her run too late. If only I'd left when Sabino was a baby – I could have kept him with me then. But it seemed that a boy should have a father.

She thought of the day, a few weeks back, when she had bumped into Victor and his sister. He had introduced Anna to his sister as an old friend. An old friend. That was one way of putting it. She had heard them laughing as they walked away. 'Old enough to be your mother,' she had heard his sister say.

She thought again of that night on the beach when they had lit the fire. The wine had been good and they had eaten hummus and pita bread. Victor had spread his red rug on the sand next to his beat-up old Kombi and they sat thigh to thigh, staring out at the ocean, talking and listening to Bob Marley as the sun slowly sank below the horizon. She remembered how he had picked her foot up and brushed the sand away as you would for a child. Something primal had moved within her at that moment.

'Anna, do you want to think things over and let me know?' said the lawyer, tucking the end of his tie into his shirt.

'Oh, yes. Yes, I'll do that,' she said. For a moment, she had forgotten he was there.

'Have one of my cards,' he said. 'Let me know what you want to do.'

'Thanks, yes, thanks,' she said. 'I'll let you know.'

Anna looked at the receptionist, once more at the Sunflowers and walked out onto the street. She thought of her husband. He wishes me dead. I know he does. That would make things so easy for him. He could keep everything. He would have Sabino and then he could just move her in. He knew that if he hung on long enough I would eventually have to crack, not be able to stand it any more. It's how I feel when I'm with him that makes it so hard. When I'm with him I feel like a non-person, like a thing, an object. Powerless.

She tried to imagine life without Sabino. She saw herself coming home to a little unit and a few silent pot plants, no teenage boy's laughter or chatter. She imagined him getting himself ready for school in the morning, joking with her husband, hardly noticing that she wasn't there. He would probably be better off without her anyway. He was always saying how sick he was of her nagging. 'Get a life, Mum!' he would say. 'Get a life!'

But he used to love her when he was little. She remembered how he would reach up and touch her cheek when she nursed him as a baby. Now he pretended he was an orphan. All teenage boys are the same, she thought. You couldn't expect him to come with you. You just have to face up to life alone. Alone. The thought was heavy in her throat. Sabino was all she had. Without him, she would be alone completely. Alone.

It's too much. Don't think of it now. I know. I'll get a cab and go and see Kathy. I'll talk to her. She'll understand. Anna pulled her compact from her bag and looked at herself and began powdering her face. Suddenly she stopped sharply and snapped the little black compact shut.

She walked down the street toward the taxi rank. She was crying now as she stood next to the cab. No, there's no point. Kathy won't understand. She never has. Why should it be any different this time? She laughs at me behind my back. She thinks that I'm a fool.

The last time she had visited, Kathy kept saying to her, 'Are you well, Anna? Are you okay? Forget about Victor and get on with the rest of your life.'

How dare she. Forget about Victor. Forget about him – that was like asking the flowers to stop growing.

Then it suddenly became clear to her what she had to do.

'I can't see you any more,' was all Victor had said. 'I can't see you any more.' No explanation. No apology. No sorrow.

Her sorrow had been bottomless, endless and terrible. Never an hour went past that she didn't think of him, still. But now if she saw him in the street, he pretended not to see her.

She thought again of the night on the beach when they had lit the fire. When the sun went down, he had pulled her under him on the red blanket and kissed her mouth and she felt him grow hard against her. She came so rapidly, with such intensity and force that she felt as if she had melted into him.

Afterwards when they were both still, she held his head in her hands and whispered over and over, as the waves lapped against the cold sand, 'Victor, I love you, I love you, I love you...'

But he was gone now. He was careless. He was gone to another. He never loved her. It was only she who loved him, she who was willing to sacrifice everything just to be with him.

She knew what she must do and walked drunkenly towards the station. Her train home was due at four o'clock.

She had that dream again last night. She was lost in the fog. She could see nothing. She was calling, 'Victor, Victor,' but she couldn't find him and she staggered about endlessly until she forced herself awake, awake and sobbing.

Yes, there was no doubt in her mind now. She could see clearly what she had to do. She was at the railway station and she was just aware of a blur of people, dark shapes, light shapes milling past her. The four o'clock train had arrived and the engine was running in readiness for departure. She walked on to the railway platform.

The world had never looked more beautiful to her than it did at that moment. It was raining softly and the sun was straining through. Everything had taken on an intense yellow glow, and the white clouds were swirling in the darkening sky. Music was coming from somewhere – soft strains of a tune her mother had hummed to her long ago, tinkling as if from a music box.

The train engine became louder. She moved closer to the edge of the platform and bent down in readiness.

'Don't... Don't...' screamed a dark-haired teenage boy running frantically along the platform.

She turned and in a split second started to run toward him. 'Sabino, Sabino, my precious.'

'Don't ... Don't... Don't go without me,' screamed the teenager as he jumped up onto the train. He knocked Anna with his skateboard. 'Sorry, lady,' he called from the carriage.

Two little girls stood staring at her, and then started to giggle behind their hands.

The train pulled away from the platform.

Anna ran from the platform and flagged down a taxi

'You okay, lady?' said the driver.

Anna was shaking uncontrollably, her face ashen, her lips blue. She sat stiffly and silently on the back seat. When the taxi stopped outside her three-bedroom, cream-brick house she blindly gave the driver all the notes in her purse and got out.

Frantically, she ran through the garden, through the front door, through the kitchen to where her son was sitting in the lounge room.

'Sabino, Sabino,' she called.

He was sitting with his back to her in front of his Playstation.

'What's up, Mum?' he said, without turning around.

Anna grabbed him and started kissing his head and hugging him fiercely.

'Geez, Mum, you've gone psycho. Leave me alone. You're messing up the game.' He pushed her away and went on with his Playstation.

Anna sat down awkwardly on the couch behind him, trying to steady herself. Her head was spinning and she was breathing hard. She heard the dull thud of her husband's work boots as he threw them on the front porch.

'Hi, Anna. What's for tea? I could eat a horse,' he said as he walked past her, ruffled Sabino's dark hair and headed toward the shower.

'*La tristesse durera toujours,*' she said hoarsely.

'Oh, okay. I don't mind a bit of French food occasionally,' her husband said.

'Mum, can I have McDonalds?' said Sabino.

'The sadness will last forever,' whispered Anna.

'Cool, Mum!'

Brother

Louis froze to death next to a burnt-out campfire in a creek bed one cold winter's morning in July.

When he heard the news, Richard wasn't shocked; somehow he had always known it would be thus. As he watched the outback sun go down over the blue-red MacDonnell Ranges, thoughts of Louis softly enveloped his mind. Leaning back against the smooth granite boulder, still warm from the heat of the long day, Richard closed his eyes and felt Louis's gentle spirit settle around him. Through the ghost gums, through the serpent rocks, through the distant dreaming of their boyhood, he heard Louis calling him.

'Hey, Pommy, wanna come to the walk-in movies tonight?'

'I'll have to ask my mam,' Richard called back in his broad Liverpool accent.

'Meet you out the front tonight,' laughed Louis, his white teeth shining as he sprinted off, his skinny black legs kicking the red dust behind him.

It was Louis who had christened him Pommy, that first week in Alice Springs, the worst week in his twelve years of life. His accent, his thick woollen baggy pants, his pale skin, his funny words, had been a source of great amusement. Only the 'coloured kids' didn't seem to care that he was different.

Louis was a 'coloured kid'. He had never met anyone from the north of England before; back then, not too many migrants made the long dusty journey to Alice Springs, the heart of the country. This strange foreigner fascinated Louis. He loved the way his cheeks seemed to break up into mottled white patches and bleed into his neck, his strange accent and his thick wet lips. He couldn't understand what he was saying at first until he got used to him, and sometimes he just liked to watch and listen while his new friend talked about his council house, train spotting, chip butties and England.

That night, Louis waited for him on the bank of the Todd River, a dry creek bed most of the time, except every once and a while when there was torrential rain and it flooded. The locals told the tourists if they saw the Todd flow they would return – such are myths and promises. At night, when the ghost gums caught the moonlight, the creek bed had a pale haunting beauty– but Louis knew that beauty could be treacherous.

Lawrence of Arabia was showing at the walk-in, open-air theatre that night. Louis and Pommy wrapped their blankets tightly around them as they sank into the cold canvas of the red and white striped deckchairs, faded and worn by the fierce sun of many long hot summers. Pommy's cheeks were glowing red in the dark from the cold; Louis's face disappeared into the thin brown blanket that he had borrowed from his bed at the children's home. Winter in the desert was cold when the sun went down.

Pommy gave him half of his chocolate bar and he ate it slowly, so as not to waste any, savouring the intoxicating sweetness. The reflection of the silver and purple paper wrapper floated in his dark eyes.

As the heroic Lawrence and the handsome dark-skinned Prince Ali charged and slaughtered their way through the hot sands of Arabia, the boys sat trance-like beneath the wide open-air screen, the reflected images disappearing into the dark night sky.

After midnight, breathing mist into the icy desert air, blankets wrapped around them like Bedouins in the night, the boys made their way along the edge of the Todd toward the bridge.

Louis knew not to walk through the creek after nightfall – too much swearing, too much fighting and too much grog – it made him scared. Shivering, he looked far into the night, through the gum trees, down the sandy creek bed and saw in the distance the smoke under the bridge.

When they reached the bridge, they parted– Louis headed north to the children's home and Pommy to his parents' home on the East Side.

Pommy knew that when he crept in the back door his mother would call out, ' Is that you, Richard darlin'? Get into your warm bed and I'll bring some hot milk – you must be dyin' of the cold.' He knew that she would lightly kiss the top of his head before he went to sleep and he would roll over and pretend to hate it.

Louis was really quiet when he got back to the home because he knew that if he woke Mrs Smith she would hit him with the rubber hose again. His bed was cold and he tucked the thin blanket tightly around his body trying to get warm. Louis closed his eyes and thought of the chocolate, his friend Pommy and the movie. Sleep closed around him and, as always, just at the moment before slumber took him completely, he saw his mother's face close to his.

***

They turned sixteen in the same year and on Louis's birthday they raced each other up Anzac Hill. Louis ran like a hare in his shoeless feet, laughing all the way while Richard struggled up the steep hill, heaving and red-faced. He hadn't even raised a sweat when he reached the top; still laughing, Louis put his fists up, shadow boxing, leaping around and dancing like a brolga under the hot summer sky. Richard sparring back was slow and clumsy. Punching the air, laughing and singing, they screamed the words of 'Don't You Tread on My Blue Suede Shoes,' until they finally collapsed together beneath the war memorial.

They fell into an easy silence as they rested at the base of the concrete pillar. You could see the whole town from the top of the hill; MacDonnell ranges to the west, Honeymoon Gap straight down the middle and Mount Gillen to the east – the parched outback landscape stretched for miles in panoramic beauty.

'Hey, Pommy, you remember that old blackfella who tried to get me for the initiation – he told me, he said that when the welfare mob came and took me, my mother, she ran off and hid in the bush for days. They could hear her wailing for three days, he said – for three days – like a wounded dog, he reckoned.'

'You might see her again one day,' said Richard.

'That old man, he reckoned she died a few years after they took me. She got drunk one night and rolled into a campfire in the creek. She wouldn't even have been thirty, so they reckon.' Then his voice falling to a whisper, 'No, broth, I won't see her again.'

Louis stared out at the over the ranges, amber in the scorching afternoon sun, out across the township and down the Todd River, and far away into the distance he could see the white haze of smoke under the bridge. His voice still in a whisper, and his eyes lowered, he said, 'I'm leaving the home next week, Pommy. Got a job – I'm going mustering at Susannah Downs.'

Richard, silent for a minute, covered his eyes, pretending to block out the sun, then wiping his face with the backs of his hands he jumped up and ran ahead calling behind him, 'Race you down. Last one down buys the smokes.'

***

Years later, Louis sat in the outpatients department of the town hospital waiting to be discharged, his eyes downcast, his check shirt sleeves rolled up above his elbows and Akubra in his hands.

'Mr Louis, please,' called the nurse, and he limped into the doctor's office on crutches, his leg in plaster.

Dressed in a purple silk sari trimmed with gold braid and smelling of honeysuckle and oranges, the doctor began to speak in a clipped superior tone. Louis fixed his eyes on the caste mark at the centre of her unlined forehead.

'So, Mr Louis, I see we have been breaking legs again. This is not good, not good at all, and as I told you last time you are well on the way to becoming a cripple. If you break your leg again, you may not walk again and you will certainly never ride a horse. Now that you are discharged, this is what you are to do. Go immediately to the government office and request that they assist you. Take this note with you.'

Her gold bangles jangled as she wrote and the folds of her skin were dark and moist. 'I hope I do not see you in this hospital again for a very long time. Good morning, Mr Louis.'

Limping slowly down the main street of the town, he made his way slowly to the government offices. The summer sun piercing his back through his shirt and the hot dusty wind in his face, he crumpled the doctor's note in his hand.

As Louis came through the door, Richard looked up. With a feeling of disbelief, he stood up from his desk and watched as Louis made his way slowly toward the counter.

As if he stepping out of a dream from some far away place of long ago, Louis, recognising him, stretched his hand across the counter and said, 'Didn't expect to see you here, broth. Long time since I've seen you. How've you been?'

'Louis, Louis, old mate, it must be years.'

It didn't matter that he was thinner and older, Richard would have known him anywhere.

'Yeah. I always wondered where you got to, Pom.'

'Jesus, the years slip by, don't they. What happened, mate? Did you get thrown off a horse?'

'Broke this one twice now and the other one the same last year.' Louis hesitated for a moment and said, 'That doctor lady at the hospital told me that if I broke it again, I'm a cripple for the rest of my life. They told me to come and see you mob. The doctor said to give you this note.'

Richard read the crumpled note and looked at him. 'Louis, you don't have to go back to the station. You can stay in town and get government money – the dole. Just until you get something sorted. All you have to do is sign the papers,' he said.

Louis was silent, his eyes glazed over and he seemed to be looking far off into the distance. The station was everything to him now – the heat, the dust, the flies, the horses, the land were his life and the closest thing that he had ever known to home

'Yeah, mate, but I reckon that dole would be the end for me – only one place I can go if I go on the dole – and you know where that is, brother. And there's no way back from there,' said Louis.

Then in a whisper he said, 'Pommy, I can't go on the dole – I've got to hang on at the station long as I can.'

The two men stared at each other in silence.

Louis knew that one day soon he would break his leg again and he would go on the dole. Then down the creek and grog, fighting and trouble. There was nothing left in town for him. Nothing.

He knew one day he would go down to the creek in the heat of the day, wait till nightfall then follow the smoke under the bridge and share the hot sherry. He knew one cold dark night his beautiful black mother would call him from the embers of a dying campfire, she would call him from his pain, call him to the dreamtime, call him to her and he would go.

Louis and Richard became locked in a gaze which knew no time or space; what passed between them at that moment was beyond friendship, beyond compassion, and in Louis's eyes, now bloodshot from the dust and flies, Richard saw his own tears and felt his own cheeks wet.

When the gaze finally broke, the two men shook hands slowly. Louis turned and limped out on his crutches.

***

The sun had set now, the stars sprinkled the black sky, and the boulder had grown cold against Richard's back. Treading the steps of their boyhood, he walked slowly home along the banks of the Todd and, pausing for a moment at the bridge, he felt the feather touch of a warm night breeze.

Such are memories and dreams. Colours, shapes and sounds change and merge with the passing of the years but the essence and the truth remain.

Sometimes now, from some distant unknown place, through the creek beds, through the Min Min lights, through the tears of the ancestors, through the years, when the moonlight is soft on the ghost gums, Richard hears the soft whisper, 'Brother, brother, brother…'

Works Cited

Page 6: Woolf, Virginia, 1928, *A Room of One's Own*.

Pages 43 & 47: Shakespeare, William, 1599, *Julius Caesar*.

Pages 56 & 58 : Van Gogh, Theo, 1890, Letter from Theo van Gogh to Elisabeth van Gogh, Paris, 5 August 1890 http:// www.webexhibits. org/vangogh/letter/21/etc-Theo-Lies.htm in compliance with the creative commons license http://creativecommons.org/licenses/by-sa/4.0/

Page 61: Tolstoy, Leo, 1878, *Anna Karenina* (translation 1901).